STRIKE FOUR!

For Ellen and Sam Margolin

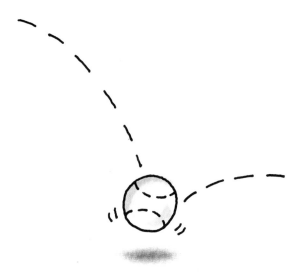

PUFFIN BOOKS
Published by the Penguin Group
Penguin Books USA Inc., 375 Hudson Street, New York, New York 10014, U.S.A.
Penguin Books Ltd, 27 Wrights Lane, London W8 5TZ, England
Penguin Books Australia Ltd, Ringwood, Victoria, Australia
Penguin Books Canada Ltd, 10 Alcorn Avenue, Toronto, Ontario, Canada M4V 3B2
Penguin Books (N.Z.) Ltd, 182-190 Wairau Road, Auckland 10, New Zealand

Penguin Books Ltd, Registered Offices: Harmondsworth, Middlesex, England

First published in the United States of America by Viking Penguin,
a division of Penguin Books USA Inc., 1988
Published simultaneously in Puffin Books
Published in a Puffin Easy-to-Read edition, 1995

3 5 7 9 10 8 6 4 2

Text copyright © Harriet Ziefert, 1988
Illustrations copyright © Mavis Smith, 1988
All rights reserved

THE LIBRARY OF CONGRESS HAS CATALOGED THE PUFFIN BOOKS EDITION AS FOLLOWS:
Ziefert, Harriet.
Strike four! (Hello reading!;)
Summary: Debbie seems to be in everyone's way as she searches for just the right place to play ball.
I. Smith, Mavis, ill. II. Title. III. Series: Ziefert, Harriet.
Hello reading! (Puffin Books);
PZ7.Z487St   1988 [E]   87-25779   ISBN 0-14-050811-2

Puffin Books ISBN 0-14-036999-6

Puffin® and Easy-to-Read® are registered trademarks of Penguin Books USA Inc.
Printed in the United States of America

Reading Level 1.6

STRIKE FOUR!

Harriet Ziefert
Pictures by Mavis Smith

PUFFIN BOOKS

Debbie had nothing to do.
So she went to her room
and found her best ball.

Debbie threw the ball.
She threw it up in the air.
And she caught it, too!

Debbie's mom said,
"Don't throw the ball here!
You'll break a lamp."

Debbie's dad said,
"Don't throw the ball here!
You'll break a window."

"Don't throw the ball here,"
said Debbie's grandpa.

"You'll wake the baby."

"Don't throw the ball in here," said Debbie's grandma.

"You'll smash the cake!"

Debbie was mad.
She dropped her ball and said,
"I can't throw near Mom!
I can't throw near Dad!
I can't throw near Grandma.
I can't throw near Grandpa.
I can't throw near the baby!
So where can I throw?"

Debbie picked up her ball.
She ran to her room.

She found her hat.

She found her bat.

Debbie ran outside.
She found a good spot
on the grass.

Debbie held the ball
in her left hand.
She held the bat
in her right hand.

Debbie threw the ball
in the air and...

she swung.
Strike one!

She threw the ball
in the air again.

She swung.
Strike two!

Debbie took one more swing.
Strike three!

And another…

STRIKE FOUR!

Debbie said, "Do you think
I'm mad? Well, I'm not!
I'm going to try again.

I'm going to hit
a home run.
Just watch me!"

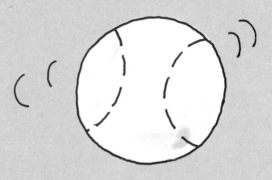

Debbie swung and...

The window broke!

The lamp fell!

The baby woke up!

But the cake
was not smashed!

Grandma said, "Oh dear,
go tell your mom and dad."

Debbie said, "I broke the window. And I'm sorry."

Dad said, "Next time
hit the ball the other way."

So Debbie did!

BENNY'S NEW FRIEND

Created by **Gertrude Chandler Warner**

Illustrated by **Daniel Mark Duffy**

Albert Whitman & Company

Morton Grove, Illinois

You will also want to read:

Meet the Boxcar Children
A Present for Grandfather

Library of Congress Cataloging-in-Publication Data

Warner, Gertrude Chandler, 1890-1979
Benny's new friend / created by Gertrude Chandler Warner;
illustrated by Daniel Mark Duffy.
p. cm.
Summary: Benny anticipates making friends with the new kid down the street,
but when he finds out that she's a girl, he is very disappointed.
ISBN 0-8075-0649-4
[1. Sex role--Fiction. 2. Friendship--Fiction. 3. Brothers and sisters--Fiction.
4. Orphans--Fiction.] I. Duffy, Daniel M., ill. II. Title.
PZ7.W244Bn   1998
[E]--dc21   98-14070
CIP
AC

Copyright © 1998 by Albert Whitman & Company.
Published in 1998 by Albert Whitman & Company,
6340 Oakton Street, Morton Grove, Illinois 60053.
Published simultaneously in Canada by
General Publishing, Limited, Toronto.

BOXCAR CHILDREN is a registered trademark
of Albert Whitman & Company.
THE ADVENTURES OF BENNY AND WATCH
is a trademark of Albert Whitman & Company.

The Boxcar Children

Henry, Jessie, Violet, and Benny Alden are orphans. They are supposed to live with their grandfather, but they have heard that he is mean. So the children run away and live in an old red boxcar. They find a dog, and Benny names him Watch.

When Grandfather finds them, the children see that he is not mean at all. They happily go to live with him. And, as a surprise, Grandfather brings the boxcar along!

The Alden family sat around the dinner
table. Watch, their dog, sat under the table
waiting for food to drop.

Henry said, "Benny, I hear a kid who's just your age moved in down the road."

"Wow," Benny said. "I'd like a new friend."

The next morning, Benny ran outside. He yelled to Jessie, "I'm going to see the new kid." He hopped on his bike. Watch ran alongside him.

When Benny reached the end of the road he
saw a child playing with a ball. Benny could
only see the back of the boy. He heard a loud
THWACK as the ball was caught.

The boy turned around. On the front
of his sweatshirt was the name BETH.
"You're a *girl*!" Benny shouted.

"So," Beth said. "What's wrong with *that*?"
"Nothing, I guess," Benny said, frowning.
"Want to play catch?" Beth asked. "Here's a mitt."
Benny put on the mitt. "I throw a pretty fast ball," he said. "Maybe too fast for you."

Beth threw the ball to Benny.
THWACK!

Benny was surprised. Beth
could throw fast, too!

Then something awful happened.
When Benny threw the ball back
to Beth, it was wide. Very wide!
Watch chased the ball and took it
to Beth.

She threw to Benny again. The
ball hit his mitt with a loud THWACK.
    But when it was Benny's turn, the
ball went wide again. Very wide!
Watch had to chase it again.

Benny threw the mitt down. "I have to go home for lunch," he said.

Beth frowned. "But it's only ten-thirty."

Benny looked away. "Well, sometimes we eat lunch early."

He got on his bike and rode
home. Watch was close behind.

That night, Henry asked, "How was the new kid?"

"He was a *girl*!" Benny said. "I don't like to play with girls."

Jessie laughed. "Well, Violet and
I are girls. You play with us."

Benny said, "You're not really *girls*.
You're just sisters."

Everyone laughed.

The next day, Benny decided to go into
the woods behind his house to pick berries.
Jessie gave him a pail and said, "Don't go too far."

The woods were cool and dark. Benny
picked the berries from the bushes. Watch
ate all the ones that fell to the ground. Benny
began to run so that Watch would chase him.

Suddenly, Benny's foot caught in a hole and he fell. When he tried to get up, he couldn't stand on his right foot. It hurt a lot. So he just sat down.

"Uh-oh. I hurt my ankle," he said to Watch. "What am I going to do? We need help."

"Help! Help!" Benny shouted. "I'm in the woods!" But there was only silence.

"Watch," Benny said. "Run home and get some help. I'll be all right here."

Benny waited and waited. Finally he heard
a noise. I hope it's not a bear, he thought.

But it wasn't. It was Watch.
And right behind him was Beth.
"What happened to you?" she asked.

Benny said, "I fell."

"That's why Watch was barking so loudly," Beth said.

Benny said proudly, "I told him to get help."

Beth looked at Benny's foot. "It's getting swollen already."

"You'll have to get Henry or Jessie to help me," Benny said.

Beth pulled something out of
her pocket. It was a mushed-up
candy bar. "Here. Keep this, in
case you get hungry." She started
to go, but quickly came back.
She put a water bottle next to him.
"Here. In case you get thirsty."
Then she left.

"Do you think she'll come back?" Benny asked Watch. "I wasn't very nice to her yesterday."

It began to get darker. And cooler. Soon, thunder rumbled in the distance, and Benny felt raindrops on his face. He shivered a little.

Soon he heard Violet's voice.
"Benny, where are you?"
Watch started barking loudly.

When Benny saw Violet and Henry
with Beth, he said, "Wow! Am I glad
to see you!"

Henry had Benny climb on his
back, and they all started home.

The next day, Benny was
playing in his room. He had been
to the doctor. The doctor had
bandaged Benny's ankle.

Benny had his collection of
baseball cards on the floor when
Beth came to the doorway.

"Are you okay?" she asked.

Benny nodded. Then he said, "I'm sure glad I sent Watch for help. A bear might have come."

Beth giggled. "Oh, Benny, there aren't any bears here!"

Beth looked at the cards. "That's a neat collection. You're sure lucky to have it."

Benny said, "I just got some new ones. Do you want to look at them with me?"

Beth said, "That's a great idea! Watch likes them, too."

Girls might not be so bad,
Benny thought.

And now I have a new friend.